W9-CDD-743

NICKELODEON®

Rugrats™

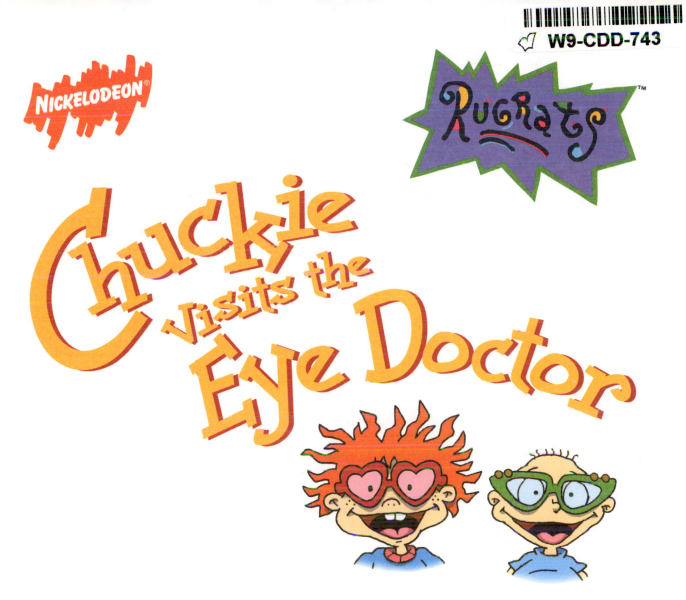

Chuckie Visits the Eye Doctor

by Luke David

illustrated by Barry Goldberg

SCHOLASTIC INC.
New York   Toronto   London   Auckland   Sydney
Mexico City   New Delhi   Hong Kong

Note to Parents

A first-time visit to the ophthalmologist can be a frightening experience, especially for young children. Read this book together to help your child express and resolve any anxiety he or she might have about an anticipated eye exam. This will help your child cope—just as Chuckie did. And if Chuckie can cope, anybody can!

KLASKY CSUPO INC.

Based on the TV series Rugrats™ created by Klasky/Csupo Inc. and Paul Germain as seen on Nickelodeon®

No part of this publication may be reproduced in whole or in part, or stored in a retrieval system, or transmitted in any form or by any means, electronic, mechanical, photocopying, recording, or otherwise, without written permission of the publisher. For information regarding permission, write to Simon Spotlight, an imprint of Simon & Schuster Children's Publishing Division, 1230 Avenue of the Americas, New York, NY 10020.

ISBN 0-439-11536-1

Copyright © 1999 by Viacom International Inc.
All rights reserved. NICKELODEON®, *Rugrats*™, and all related titles, logos, and characters are trademarks of Viacom International Inc. Published by Scholastic Inc., 555 Broadway, New York, NY 10012, by arrangement with Simon Spotlight, an imprint of Simon & Schuster Children's Publishing Division. SCHOLASTIC and associated logos are trademarks and/or registered trademarks of Scholastic Inc.

12 11 10 9 8 7 6 5 4 3 2 1   9/9 0 1 2 3 4/0

Printed in the U.S.A.   23

First Scholastic printing, December 1999

One morning a long time ago, Tommy and Chuckie were playing Reptar. "Rrrrr! Rrrrr!" growled Tommy. He held his Reptar at arm's length and shook him fiercely.

Chuckie held his Reptar close to his face and squinted. "Rrrrr-rrrrr?" he said.

Next Tommy and Chuckie played tag. Chuckie was it. "Got you!" said Chuckie as he reached to tag an armchair. *Wumpf!* Chuckie bumped into the footstool. "I thought the chair was you, Tommy!" laughed Chuckie. He picked himself up.

"You're still it, Chuckie," said Tommy, giggling. "Try to get me."

Then Chuckie tried to tag the TV. *Clonk!* Chuckie tripped and fell. "Ouch!" said Chuckie. "I got a boo-boo on my head. I don't think I like this game, Tommy."

"Okay," said Tommy. "Let's do something else."

Just then Stu walked in. "*Dummi Bears* is on, boys." *Zap!* He turned on the TV. Tommy and Chuckie sat together on the floor to watch.

"I can't see," said Chuckie. He scooted forward. "I still can't see too well," he said. He scooted forward again. "That's better." Chuckie was sitting smack in front of the screen.

"Whoa now, buddy," said Stu. "You're too close." He picked Chuckie up and moved him back. Chuckie started to cry.

"Aw, don't cry, Chuckie," pleaded Stu. "Y'know what? It's too nice a day to be cooped up in here. Let's go outside and play in the backyard."

Chuckie could hear his dad and Tommy's mom talking.

"It's awfully nice of you to help me aerate the lawn, Chas," said Didi.

"My pleasure," replied Chas. Then he saw the babies coming. "Hey, Chuckie, come to Dad!"

Chuckie toddled across the grass toward Chas.

Chuckie toddled right into a small tree. *Thud!* He was knocked flat on his behind.

"Oops!" said Chuckie.

Chas picked Chuckie up and hugged him. "Poor little guy! Funny, but that used to happen to me all the time before I got my glasses. . . ."

"Chas?" Didi asked gently. "Do you think maybe it's time for Chuckie to get his own pair of glasses?"

"He was sitting smack in front of the TV, as if he couldn't see," added Stu.

Chas nodded. "Y'know, I was just about Chuckie's age when I got my first pair of glasses. I'll call right away for an appointment at the eye doctor."

"TOMMY!" said Chuckie. "The regular doctor is bad enough. Just think how scary an eye doctor must be!"

"It might not be so bad, Chuckie," said Tommy. "Remember how I didn't want to get my rooster shot, but then in the end it didn't hurt at all, and the doctor gave me a lollipop?"

"Maybe your rooster shot didn't hurt, but mine scared the poop out of me!" said Chuckie.

"The eye doctor can squeeze us in this afternoon, Chuckie," said Chas. "Don't worry, son. Wearing glasses isn't so bad. Lots of people do. I do and so does Tommy's Grandpa."

"Conflabbit!" said Grandpa Lou. "I feel like a human windshield wiper. Why, it took me *fifteen* years to get used to wearing glasses."

"Don't mind him, Chuckie," said Chas. "It's fun to wear glasses. They help you see everything better. Didi, is it okay if Tommy comes with us to make Chuckie more comfortable?"

"Of course," said Didi. "It will be educational for Tommy."

"Nice to meet you, Chuckie," said Dr. Pedop. "You can sit here, right between your dad and your friend."

"See!" whispered Tommy. "She looks nice."

"First let's test your dad's eyes," Dr. Pedop beamed a tiny flashlight right into one of Chas's eyes, then into the other. Chas smiled.

"Okay, Chuckie," continued the doctor, "you and Tommy can try the lights on each other." Tommy and Chuckie zapped the lights on each other's face. They giggled.

"Now I'll try it on you, Chuckie," said the doctor.

"It doesn't hurt at all, Tommy," whispered Chuckie.

"Now, Chas, you read the chart," said Dr. Pedop. "I'll point to one of these big E's and you use your finger to show me which way it's pointing."

"Now it's your turn, Chuckie."

"Okay, see this cool machine? It's like a pair of binoculars, but instead of looking at something far away, we use it to look at eyes up close," explained Dr. Pedop. "You try it on your friend, Chuckie, and then I'll try it on you."

"You did really well, Chuckie!" said the doctor. "The good news is that you're going to get an extra pair of eyes. They're called glasses, and lots of people wear them. Now, would you and your friend like lollipops?"

"Chuckie, I'm so proud of you! You were a brave boy during that eye exam," said Chas. "And, Tommy, thanks so much for helping Chuckie."

"And now for the fun part, Chuckie," said his dad. "You get to pick out your own frames!"

"You know what, Tommy?" said Chuckie. "It wasn't that bad after all. Glasses make everything look better!"